Kane/Miller Book Publishers, Inc.
First American Edition 2008
by Kane/Miller Book Publishers, Inc.
La Jolla, California

AHIRU NO HANNAH by Anji Yamamura
Copyright © Anji Yamamura 2005
Original Japanese edition published by Singpoosha Publishing Co.
This English edition is published by arrangement with Singpoosha Publishing Co., Tokyo
in care of Tuttle-Mori Agency, Inc., Tokyo

Kane/Miller Book Publishers, Inc.
P.O. Box 8515
La Jolla, CA 92038
www.kanemiller.com

Library of Congress Control Number: 2007932690
Printed and bound in China
1 2 3 4 5 6 7 8 9 10

ISBN: 978-1-933605-74-6

Hannah Duck

By Anji Yamamura

Kane/Miller
BOOK PUBLISHERS

Most days, Hannah Duck felt peaceful and content, happy at home
with Gigi the parakeet and KameKame the turtle.

On Sundays, Hannah Duck
went for a walk.
"See you later!"

She tried to hide it, but Hannah Duck was not peaceful and content on Sundays.

Every Sunday, Hannah Duck walked to the park. And every Sunday she stopped, and looked through the gate.

And then, every Sunday, Hannah Duck turned around, and went home.

Gigi and KameKame were always waiting to hear about her walk. Hannah Duck took a deep breath…

"I'm back!"

Gigi was full of questions.
"How was it? Did you have a good time?
What did you do? Who did you see?"

Then it was KameKame's turn.
"How was the sun? Was it warm?"

It was always the same.

Then one day, Hannah Duck had enough pretending.
"Gigi, I'm not going on any more walks. The truth is…"
Hannah Duck started, then stopped. This was hard.
"I don't like walks. They scare me."

"Well," said Gigi, thinking carefully, "what if I come with you?"

The next Sunday, when Hannah Duck stopped at the park gate, Gigi was full of encouragement.

"You can do it, Hannah Duck. I'm right here."

Hannah Duck found her courage. She looked at Gigi, and stepped through the gate, into the park.

"Hello dears! Lovely day!" called the pigeons. They were very nice.

The sun was warm, and the crows nodded
and smiled hello.
"Hello," Hannah Duck smiled back.
"Beautiful day," said the cats.
Everyone was so friendly.

"Gigi? Gigi!"
She looked up at the
sky, to find Gigi and…

"It is, isn't it, Gigi?"
cried Hannah Duck.
"It's a beautiful day
in the park!"

...the most beautiful sunset she'd ever seen.

The sun was almost gone, and
the air was growing cooler.
But Hannah Duck felt
warm inside, as she and
Gigi walked slowly home.

"We're back!"
"You were gone so long,"
said KameKame.
"Did you have a good time?"

"Yes," said Hannah Duck, "but maybe next time, you should come too."

And from then on Hannah Duck, Gigi the parakeet and KameKame the turtle were peaceful and content every day.

Including Sundays.